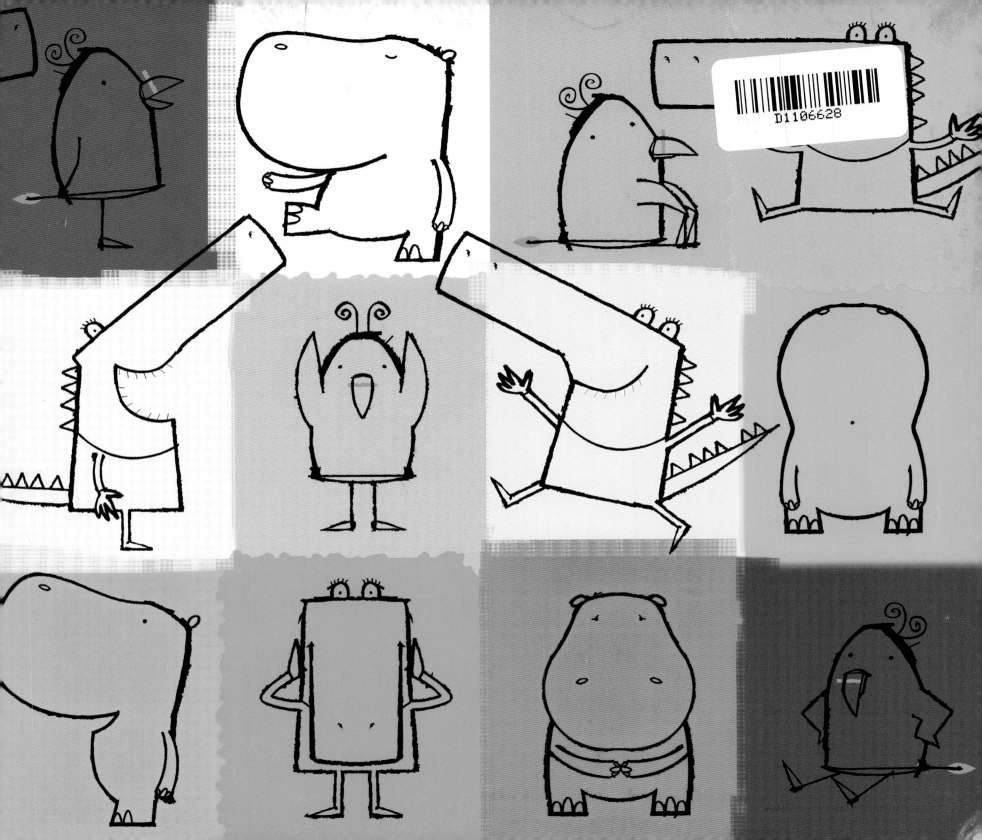

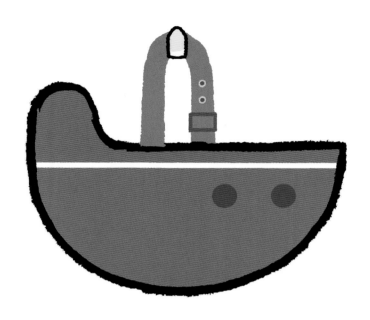

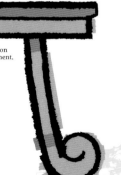

For friends,
old and new.
A.B.

For Erin
and Isla
S.R.

OXFORD
UNIVERSITY PRESS

Great Clarendon Street, Oxford OX2 6DP

Oxford University Press is a department of the University of Oxford.
It furthers the University's objective of excellence in research,
scholarship,
and education by publishing worldwide in

Oxford New York

Auckland Cape Town Dar es Salaam Hong Kong Karachi
Kuala Lumpur Madrid Melbourne Mexico City Nairobi
New Delhi Shanghai Taipei Toronto

With offices in

Argentina Austria Brazil Chile Czech Republic France Greece
Guatemala Hungary Italy Japan Poland Portugal Singapore

South Korea Switzerland Thailand Turkey Ukraine Vietnam

Oxford is a registered trade mark of Oxford University Press
in the UK and in certain other countries

Text © Ann Bonwill 2014
Illustrations © Simon Rickerty 2014
Photograph on page 4 © Graeme Shannon/Shutterstock.com

The moral rights of the author/illustrator have been asserted

Database right Oxford University Press (maker)

First published in 2014

British Library Cataloguing in Publication Data available

ISBN: 978-0-19-273499-0 (hardback)
ISBN: 978-0-19-273500-3 (paperback)

2 4 6 8 10 9 7 5 3 1

Printed in China

Paper used in the production of this book is a natural,
recyclable product made from wood grown in sustainable forests.
The manufacturing process conforms to the environmental
regulations of the country of origin

I totally don't want to play!

featuring **Hugo,**
Bella, and
Cressida!

Ann Bonwill &
Simon Rickerty

OXFORD
UNIVERSITY PRESS

Hello, Bella, are you ready to go skating?

Sorry, Hugo, skating slipped my mind. I'm going to the playground with Cressida.

Cressida?

Yes, Cressida.
She's my fabulous
new friend!

But Bella, we **always** go skating together.

Embrace change, Hugo. Come to the playground with us. It's bound to be fun with Cressida around.

Supremely fun!

Let me know when the fun starts.

Swings! How I love the feel of the wind in my hair . . .

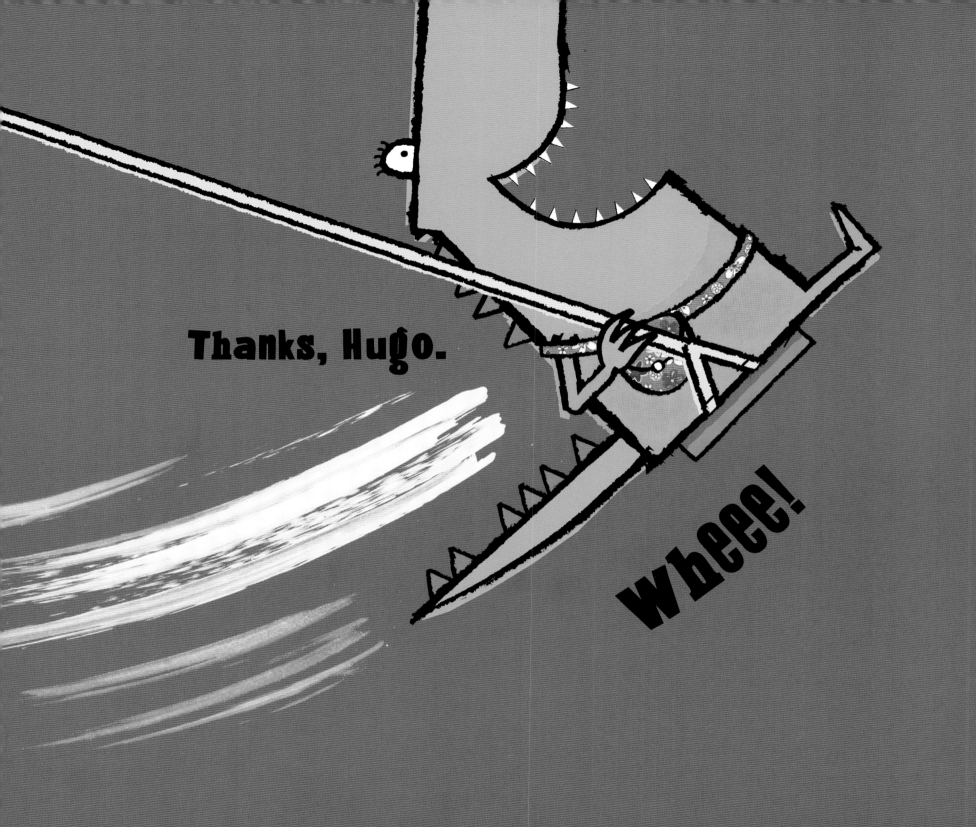

My
turn
now.
Who's
going
to
push
me?

Sorry, Hugo.
There's a see-saw
over there that's
just perfect for
Cressida and me.

Hmmm. Something's not quite right.

Very true. Hugo, come and see-saw with me!

You mean leap-croc!

Wait for me . . .

Ow! I totally don't want
to play any more.

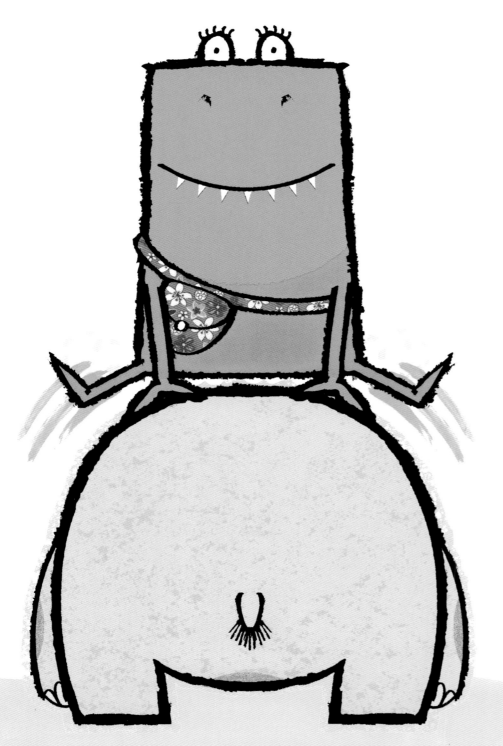

This playground isn't made for three. I'm going home.

we are   three

friends together!